# GREAT ILLUSTRATED CLASSICS

# WHITE FANG

### Jack London

**adapted by
Malvina G. Vogel**

**Illustrations by
Ross Vera**

BARONET BOOKS, New York, New York

# GREAT ILLUSTRATED CLASSICS

### edited by
### Joshua E. Hanft

# Contents

## About the Author

Jack London lived in the slums of Oakland, California, from the time of his birth in 1876 until his teen years. With no prospect for the future and always in trouble, Jack left home and worked at many jobs all over the world. He slaved in a cannery, pirated oysters, shoveled coal, trapped seals in the Bering Sea, and crossed America as a hobo. This resulted in his arrest and jailing in Niagara Falls, N. Y.

After his release, London realized that the only way to make a success of his life was to improve his mind, not his muscles. So he returned to California to finish high school, then start college. After winning a newspaper story contest, London decided that writing was his road to fame and fortune. But in 1897, he caught the gold fever that was sweeping the nation and left school to travel to Alaska and the Klondike.

While he found no gold and returned to California penniless, he found something more precious than gold—he found his writing inspiration in the cold North and in his experiences with dogs and wolves. These animals made such an impression on London that they became the heroes of two of his most popular stories, *The Call of the Wild* and *White Fang*. He even gave himself the nickname "Wolf," later named his large California mansion "Wolf House," and had a wolf-dog engraved on his bookmarks.

During his sixteen-year writing career, Jack London produced an amazing number of works: nineteen novels, eighteen collections of essays and short stories, and many other books. Though a world-famous millionaire, London was constantly in debt from spending more than he earned.

By the time he was forty, Jack London was just a shadow of his former vigorous, energetic self; he fell victim to several illnesses that wasted his strength and eventually broke him, but not before he had written his classic tales of action and adventure that have thrilled generations of readers.

Eyes Like Hot Coals

# CHAPTER 1

## The Starving Wolf Pack

The eyes of the starving wolf pack gleamed like hot coals in the blackness of the frozen Arctic forest. They stared hungrily at the two man-animals and their dog-sled team huddled around the campfire. These man-animals had fish and they had meat. To a starving wolf pack, who had had little to eat in months, the dogs and the man-animals themselves were meat, too.

So the pack had been trailing behind the man-animals and their team for many days now, daring to come close only at night, when

7

everyone was asleep and the fire had died down.

Only one wolf—the part-wolf, part-dog who had once been called Kiche—knew the ways of man-animals. Because she looked so much like a husky sled-dog—five feet long and two and a half feet high at her shoulders—Kiche had been daring enough to enter the camp many times when the men were tossing fish to the dogs and get one for herself. But one fish wasn't enough for her and certainly not enough for the starving, emaciated pack.

So Kiche began using her intelligence and her cunning to silently steal into the camp and lure the male dogs, one at a time, into the woods. She would trot up to a dog, sniff noses with him, then step back, playfully encouraging him to come closer. With each step the male took, Kiche would retreat a step until the dog found himself surrounded by dozens of snarling, attacking wolves.

Night after night, Kiche lured the dogs into

Only Kiche knew the Ways of Man-Animals.

the woods until only one of the seven in the team remained. It was only then that the man-animal named Bill panicked. He had had enough!

He lay awake that night and followed Kiche and his last sled-dog into the woods. But his rifle was no match for the starving wolves, and the last sound his partner Henry heard was Bill's gasping shrieks of terror.

For the next several nights, Henry kept the wolves away by keeping his fire burning and by flinging flaming coals at them. But this meant that Henry couldn't sleep; he couldn't dare let the fire go out.

By day, the wolf pack continued to follow Henry's trail. They were weak from starvation, and it was a wonder that they didn't just collapse in the snow. Their thin skins stretched over their bony frames and their red tongues drooped limply from their jaws. But with only one man-animal to face, the pack became much bolder, coming closer and

Kiche Lured the Dogs into the Woods.

closer to him each night, even with the campfire burning.

Henry couldn't stay awake much longer. He had gone without sleep for days, and he was beginning to fear that he himself would be the wolf pack's next meal. Sitting beside his campfire, inside a larger circle of fire to keep the wolves away, Henry felt his head begin to droop and his eyes begin to close.

Kiche had been watching intently, and she now led the howling pack to the edge of the circle and, in a leap, through the dying fire.

Henry panicked as he awoke to find wolves all about him and on top of him. One had closed on his arm, while another was tearing into his leg. He would, indeed, have become the pack's next meal if the sound of man-animal voices and barking dogs hadn't reached Kiche's alert ears. And it was she who led the reluctant pack away from the meal that Henry was to have been.

Without Sleep for Days

Leading the pack with Kiche was an old, scarred male wolf with one eye. Even in his starved, weakened condition, his experience and wisdom had helped him fight off younger and stronger rivals for his position as the pack leader and Kiche's mate.

Now, at the head of their pack of forty wolves, Kiche and One Eye led the search for food over the frozen ground for many days and nights. Finally, they came upon a huge bull moose weighing over eight hundred pounds.

Although the moose fought desperately with his hooves and antlers, forty wolves coming at him from all sides were too much. Soon, twenty pounds of moose meat filled each wolf's belly, and the satisfied pack rested.

Now that they had reached a land where game was plentiful, the pack began to scatter in different directions. Kiche and One Eye headed for the Mackenzie River, where

Kiche and One Eye Led the Search for Food.

Kiche spent much of her time searching under fallen trees, in snow-covered crevices in rocks, and in caves along the banks of the river. One Eye had no interest in Kiche's search, but he followed her and waited patiently until she was ready to go on.

One night, the two wolves reached a large open space in the forest. It was an Indian camp. Sounds of dogs barking, men shouting, women scolding, and children crying mixed with sights of tepees and campfires and smells of food cooking. These sounds and sights and smells were new to One Eye, but very familiar to Kiche.

The she-wolf wanted to go closer to the fire, to be with the dogs and men. But then she realized that the need to continue her search was more urgent, so she turned and trotted back into the forest.

The Wolves Reached an Indian Camp.

Time to Find the Right Place

# CHAPTER 2

## A New Wolf Family

By the time the two wolves had traveled several days past the Indian camp, Kiche was running very slowly. She knew that it was time to find the right place to give birth to her cubs.

She found that place in a small cave alongside a frozen stream. She sniffed around, inspecting the ground, then circled one spot several times before dropping down with a tired sigh.

One Eye dozed peacefully outside in the April sunshine. He had no idea why Kiche was inside the cave. It wasn't until hours later that faint, strange sounds from inside roused his curiosity.

He got up and trotted into the cave, only to be forced back by Kiche's snarls. Curled up against her were five helpless, little cubs, all making tiny, whimpering noises. This was not the first time that One Eye had become a father, but each time it was a pleasant surprise to him.

For Kiche, having cubs was a first-time experience. Her instinct was like any mother's, and she knew exactly what to do to care for them. Her instinct also made her guard her cubs even against One Eye, since wolf fathers were known to eat their helpless newborn.

But there was no danger from One Eye. His instincts had prepared him to leave his mate alone to care for the cubs and to go out and find food for his family.

He followed the stream outside the cave for

Curled Up Against Her Were Five Cubs.

several hours when he came upon a ptarmigan sitting on a log. The slow-witted bird became a tasty meal for One Eye. But he had even greater luck in finding meat for his family when he came upon a porcupine lying on the ground, killed in a fight with a female lynx. One Eye arrived on the scene in time to see the lynx fleeing, screaming from the porcupine's quills embedded in her nose.

One Eye crept up to the dead porcupine, carefully gripped it with his teeth, then set off on the trail to the cave, dragging the porcupine home to his family.

Kiche greeted One Eye with a lick on the neck to thank him for the meal, then warned him away from the cubs with a snarl. But she was not as frightened of her mate as she had been earlier. After all, he was behaving as a wolf father should in providing food for his family, and he was not showing any desire to eat her cubs.

**Kiche Greeted One Eye.**

The Fifth Cub Looked Like a True Wolf.

# CHAPTER 3

## The Gray Cub Explores His World

Of the five cubs in the litter, four had inherited Kiche's doglike reddish fur. The fifth, a little gray cub, looked like the true wolf that his father was.

Even before his eyes were opened, the little gray cub could feel and taste and smell. He knew his brothers and sisters, and romped with them. He knew his mother by her touch and taste and smell, by the milk she gave him, and by her gentle tongue that caressed his soft little body as he snuggled against her to go to sleep.

# WHITE FANG

After the first month, when his eyes were open, the cub began to explore his world. There wasn't much to see on the three dark walls that he kept bumping into, and his mother nudged him back with her nose or her paw from the light on the fourth wall. He couldn't understand how his father could walk through that wall and just disappear!

As the little gray cub's body grew, so did his wolflike ferocity. He growled louder than his brothers and sisters; his rages were more terrible; he was the first to roll them over with a slap of his paw, and he was punished the most for exploring the wall of light at the cave entrance.

The cub also had the sad experience of learning what hunger was. There came a time when his mother had no meat to chew up and feed to him and no milk to give him from her breast. One Eye went out hunting every day, but came back with nothing for his family. A terrible famine had hit the land!

His Rages Were More Terrible.

At first, the cubs whimpered and cried, then they slept. It was a long, hungry sleep, and his brothers and sisters never woke up. Only the gray cub survived.

When the famine ended and Kiche began feeding her little gray cub again, he quickly regained his strength. But now it was the she-wolf who went out hunting, for Kiche had found the remains of her mate on the trail near a lynx's lair.

With his mother out hunting, the cub's growing curiosity led him to disobey her and go through the wall of light. How bewildered the cub was as he gazed at the mountains, the sky, and the trees!

The flat floor of the cave had been the only ground beneath his tiny legs, so he wasn't prepared for the drop at the cave entrance. He stepped boldly out, only to tumble forward and roll down the slope. This hard unknown thing was hurting him, and he yelped like any frightened puppy until he came to a stop

How Bewildered the Cub Was!

in some soft grass.

He sat up and gazed around him. He wasn't hurt. This surprised him. But a squirrel hurrying by terrified him. He crouched down and snarled, but the squirrel ran up a tree and began to chatter down at him.

The next living creature he saw was a woodpecker. Although the bird startled him, the cub was developing his courage. So he just ignored the bird and continued on his way. His meeting with a moosebird, however, brought him a storm of pecks on the end of his nose, and he yelped in pain.

A ptarmigan nest inside a rotted tree trunk fascinated him. And the seven chicks inside made a tasty meal.

As he was licking his chops and preparing to go on his way, the ptarmigan mother flew down in a rage and began beating him with her wings. At first, he hid his head between his paws and yelped. Then he struck out at her with his paws and sank his teeth into one

The Mother Flew Down in a Rage.

of her wings. This was the cub's first battle and he was overjoyed. He forgot fear as the fight went on; he knew only that this bird was meat and wolves killed meat to eat.

But the battle was too much. After several minutes, they both stopped struggling and lay on the ground looking at each other. The bird's wing was still in the cub's mouth, and she began pecking at his nose to free it. His nose was still sore from the moose-bird's pecks and he finally had to let go of the wing.

As the cub scampered away, he saw a large hawk swoop down silently, bury its claws in the ptarmigan, and carry the small, squawking bird up into the sky. Seeing the hawk capture the ptarmigan taught the cub the wisdom of staying away from any creature larger than himself.

When the birds were out of sight and his courage had returned, the cub continued on until he came to a stream. He had never seen

Seeing the Hawk Capture the Ptarmigan

water, but it looked smooth and flat, not like the slope he had rolled down. So he stepped boldly onto it, only to go down and under. It was cold and he was terrified. He tried to catch his breath, but water rushed into his lungs.

He came to the surface and gasped for air. Although he had never learned to swim, his instinct told him to move his legs to stay afloat. He headed for the bank, but the swift current began to sweep him downstream. He was tossed against rocks and pulled under the water again and again before he reached the bank and crawled out.

He had learned another lesson. Water was not alive, but it moved. It looked solid, but it wasn't. So things were not always as they appeared.

At that moment, the cub's little body and little brain reminded him that they were tired. Right now, he wanted his mother more than he wanted anything else in the world.

Water Rushed into His Lungs.

So he set out to find his cave. He hadn't gone far when a small yellow weasel leaped in front of him, then disappeared into the bushes. It was soon followed by a baby weasel a few inches long. The cub reached out his paw and turned the weasel over. Its odd, grating noise brought the mother weasel back in an instant. She attacked the cub with a blow to his neck, and bit into his flesh, digging her teeth deep into his throat.

The cub snarled and struggled to escape, but he could only whimper. He would have been killed in moments if his mother hadn't come bounding through the bushes to attack the weasel. With a snap of her jaws, Kiche broke the weasel's hold. Then she flung the attacker high into the air and waited for it to come down into her open mouth.

Kiche nuzzled her cub and licked his wounds. Then the two ate the weasel and returned to their cave for a peaceful, contented sleep.

He Would Have Been Killed in Moments.

She Was Not Afraid of Anything.

# CHAPTER 4

## Eat or Be Eaten!

As the days and weeks passed, the cub went farther and farther from the cave, learning his strengths and his weaknesses, learning when to be bold and when to be cautious, when to run swiftly and when to slink furtively. He began catching ptarmigans and squirrels and moosebirds as he became more and more like his mother.

The cub was developing a great respect for her, for she was not afraid of anything. She was a powerful creature, and he knew he had to obey her.

But famine came to their land again, and Kiche ran herself thin searching for meat. Before, the cub had hunted just for fun, but now he searched for food as hungrily as his mother did. Sadly, he too found none. But he was learning to be smart and carefully to study the habits of small forest animals and birds. This helped him catch some for a small meal and gave him more confidence in himself.

When Kiche brought home a lynx kitten just for him, the cub understood that the famine was over. Kiche didn't eat any of the kitten herself, so the cub guessed that she had found something else to satisfy her. What he couldn't know was that his mother's stomach was filled with the rest of the lynx litter. Nor could he know that Kiche was so desperate to get food that she dared enter a mother lynx's lair and take her kittens.

But a lynx mother is a raging demon when her kittens are harmed, and a while later her

Now He Searched Hungrily.

terrible snarling reached the cub's ears as he dozed peacefully beside Kiche.

The lynx rushed into the cave, raging at Kiche. There were terrible snarls and spitting and screeching as the two animals began ripping and tearing at each other. Even the cub got into the fight by sinking his teeth into the lynx's hind leg. But the lynx lashed out with her huge paw, ripping open the cub's shoulder and flinging him against the cave wall.

When the fight was finally over, the lynx lay dead and Kiche was badly wounded. Even though she had lost a great deal of blood, she still caressed her cub and licked his wounded shoulder.

For a day and night Kiche lay still. She was hardly breathing. For a week, she never left the cave except to get water. By then, mother and cub had eaten the lynx and Kiche was well enough to go out hunting again.

The cub's shoulder was stiff and sore, but he

Two Animals Tearing at Each Other.

had a changed air about him. He had been in a fight, he had buried his teeth into an enemy... and he had survived! How bold he felt now! So bold that he began accompanying his mother on the trail and learning a wolf's hunting ways.

He was also learning that life depended on meat and that the law in the Wild was EAT OR BE EATEN. He had learned that lesson well with ptarmigans and hawks and weasels and lynxes. He had learned the thrills and terrors of battle. He had learned the joys of victory and the satisfaction of a full stomach. He was alive and happy and proud of himself!

Alive and Happy and Proud!

The Wolf-Cub's First Look at Man.

# CHAPTER 5

# Man-Animals ... Gods!

It was the cub's usual habit to wake from a deep sleep and run down his familiar trail through the woods to drink at a small pool. But one morning, he knew something was different when he entered the woods a different sight and a different smell.

Before him, sitting on their haunches, were five living things, things he had never seen before. It was the wolf-cub's first look at man.

When these living things saw him, they didn't spring to their feet or show their teeth or snarl like other living things did. They just sat and silently stared at him.

The cub stopped and stared back. Normally, he would have run swiftly away, but a strong instinct told him that these two-legged creatures, these Indians, were more powerful than any other animal he had ever known.

One of the Indians rose and walked over to the cub. He raised his hand and stooped over. The frightened cub cowered close to the ground. His hair bristled and his lips trembled, baring his little fangs.

The man pointed to the cub as he laughed and said, *"Wabam wabisca ip pit tah."* ("Look! The white fangs!")

The other Indians laughed loudly and urged the man to pick up the cub. As he brought his hand down, the little cub was ready to fight. He waited until the hand was almost on him, then he snapped his teeth into it.

The next moment, a hard smack on his head knocked the cub over on his side. Fear

The Cub Was Ready to Fight.

took the place of fight, and he sat up on his haunches, trembling and yelping.

The Indians surrounded the cub, still laughing at him. Even the man who had been bitten was laughing. And all the cub could do was wail out his terror and his hurt.

But in the midst of his wailing, he heard a familiar sound. His mother was coming to save him—his ferocious, powerful mother who wasn't afraid of anything!

Kiche bounded in and stood over her cub, snarling her rage at the Indians as they backed away.

Suddenly, a cry of surprise went up from one of the Indians. "Kiche?" Then he said the name again, as a sharp command. "Kiche!"

The cub saw his mother crouch down until her belly touched the ground. She was whimpering and wagging her tail. The cub was puzzled. Did his mother fear these man-animals? Did she know their power?

The man who had called out Kiche's name

His Mother Was Coming to Save Him!

came over and put his hand on her head. She didn't snap or snarl. The other men did the same, and again Kiche let them touch her.

"Kiche's mother was my brother's dog," explained Gray Beaver, the Indian who had recognized her. "She mated with a wolf some years ago, and Kiche was the result. But last year, Kiche ran away from my brother, but with good reason. We had a famine, and there was no meat for any of the dogs.

"Kiche probably went to live with the wolves and mated with one, just like her mother. This little cub is the result of that mating. He is part-dog and part-wolf, but more wolf than dog. His fangs are white, so I shall name him White Fang. And he will be my dog since my brother is dead."

Then Gray Beaver cut a branch from a tree and fastened strings of rawhide at each end. He tied one string around Kiche's throat and the other to a small pine tree.

White Fang followed his mother and lay

Kiche Let Them Touch Her.

down beside her. Gray Beaver rolled him over on his back and began to rub his stomach playfully. This frightened White Fang, for he was helpless on his back with his feet up in the air, but he found that the rubbing was a pleasant feeling, so he didn't growl at it.

Soon, White Fang heard more man-animal noises and saw the rest of the tribe coming: forty men, women, and children, plus many dogs, all carrying the tribe's belongings.

White Fang had never seen dogs before. At first, his instinct told him they were like him, but he soon learned that they were very unfriendly. They rushed at him and at Kiche, slashing at them with their teeth.

Kiche tried desperately to defend her cub. Even White Fang bit and tore at the bellies of the dogs above him. But with Kiche tied up and all the dogs on top of them, they were defenseless. It wasn't until the man-animals came at the dogs with their clubs and stones that they were driven back.

They Rushed at Him and Kiche.

At that moment, White Fang realized that these man-animals were powerful. They made the laws and carried them out. They didn't bite or claw the way other animals did; they used the power of dead things, like sticks and stones, making them leap through the air to hurt and punish the dogs. To White Fang, this was an unusual power... a godlike power!

Taking only a little time to lick his wounds, White Fang was soon up and walking. He followed behind his mother, who was now being led by her stick in the hands of a tiny man-animal called Mit-sah, who was Gray Beaver's son.

Kiche and White Fang became part of the tribe that was marching into a valley that opened into the Mackenzie River.

At their campsite, White Fang watched in wonder as the Indians stuck poles in the ground and covered them with cloth and skins. Surely, these monstrous forms, these tepees that grew out of the earth in only

Kiche and White Fang Became Part of the Tribe.

minutes, were frightful things. But after seeing the women and children go in and come out of these forms without being harmed, White Fang knew he had nothing to fear.

Although he saw dogs being chased away from the tepees by loud noises from the women and by flying stones from the children, White Fang's curiosity couldn't keep him away. He left Kiche's side and crawled slowly to a tepee. His nose smelled the cloth and his teeth bit down on it. Then he began to tug. Soon, the whole tepee was moving... moving... moving until the sharp cry of the squaw inside sent White Fang hurrying back to his mother.

But the next moment he was straying again. This time it was to make friends with a puppy called Lip-lip. But this larger and older puppy was snarling and bristling as he came toward White Fang. So the wolf-cub did the same, thinking it was some sort of a puppy game.

Soon the Whole Teepee Was Moving...

Then suddenly, Lip-lip leaped at White Fang and snapped at the shoulder that had been injured by the lynx. Life at the Indian camp had prepared Lip-lip for fighting with other puppies, and his sharp little teeth cut into White Fang many times before the cub fled to his mother, yelping shamelessly.

After a few minutes of soothing by Kiche's tongue, White Fang was off exploring again. This time, he found Gray Beaver doing something on the ground with a pile of sticks and dry moss. Soon, a strange cloud rose up. Then that cloud turned into a twisting, living thing, the color of the sun.

White Fang knew nothing about fire, but he was attracted to the light. He crawled closer to the flame and stuck his little tongue and nose out to reach it.

For a moment he was paralyzed, then he scrambled backward, yelping his cries of pain. Hearing her cub's cries, Kiche pulled at her stick in a rage, helpless to come to White

Lip-Lip Leaped at White Fang.

Fang's aid.

Gray Beaver laughed loudly and called everyone to see White Fang. Soon, they were all laughing at the pitiful little cub who sat yelping and crying and trying to soothe his burnt nose with his burnt tongue.

At that moment, White Fang understood what shame was. He knew the Indians were laughing at him, and he couldn't bear it. He turned and fled to his mother. He fled, not from the hurt of the fire, but from the laughter of the man-animals, which hurt even more.

Lying at his mother's side, White Fang understood that he couldn't do anything about the man-animals' laughter. He also knew that they had wondrous powers. They could move dead things through the air, and they could make dead moss and sticks come alive. They were fire-makers! They were gods!

Laughing at the Pitiful Little Cub

**Lip-Lip Was the Worst Torment.**

# CHAPTER 6

## The Ferocious, Intelligent Outcast

As the days and weeks passed, White Fang learned to obey the man-animals. When they called, he came. When they walked, he got out of their way. When they ordered him to go, he went. He knew that these gods had the power to hurt him, so he obeyed.

But when it was the dogs who hurt him, White Fang was confused. Lip-lip was a bully and became the worst torment of the cub's life. Whenever White Fang left Kiche's side, the older puppy followed him, waiting until no man-animal was watching to spring on the cub and force a fight, a fight which Lip-lip always won.

In spite of all these defeats, White Fang didn't lose his spirit. He couldn't frolic and play with the other puppies because Lip-lip drove him away. While he was no longer the happy, playful cub he once was, he was still a fighter, and an intelligent one too. He spent his time developing his mind, and becoming sly and cunning enough to one day get his revenge on Lip-lip.

The beginning of that revenge came on a day when White Fang was able to lure Lip-lip away from the other dogs. Just as Kiche had lured the sled dogs from Henry and Bill's camp long ago, White Fang lured Lip-lip. He led him on a wild chase, in and out and around the tepees, until he had led the bully right into Kiche's avenging jaws.

Although Kiche was still tied up, she rolled Lip-lip onto the ground and ripped and slashed at him with her fangs. When the dog

He Led Him on a Wild Chase.

finally managed to roll free, wounded and wailing, White Fang rushed in and sank his tiny wolf teeth into the dog's leg. With no fight left in him, Lip-lip ran away.

The day finally came when Gray Beaver decided that Kiche could be trusted to not run away, so he untied her. White Fang was at her side as she trotted off toward the woods. When she stopped at the edge, White Fang began whining and licking her face, pleading with her to go farther, to return to the freedom of the Wild.

But the power of the gods was too strong in Kiche, and she turned and slowly trotted back to camp. White Fang still needed his mother more than he needed his freedom, so he sadly trailed along after her.

But the man-animals didn't care that the wolf-cub needed his mother. And since Gray Beaver owed a debt to his tribesman, Three Eagles, he paid it by giving Kiche to him.

Three Eagles was going on a trip up the

Kiche Could Be Trusted.

# WHITE FANG

Mackenzie River and was putting Kiche into his canoe. White Fang saw this and tried to get in the canoe with her, but Three Eagles threw him back onto the shore.

As the canoe shoved off, the terrified cub jumped into the water to follow his mother. He ignored Gray Beaver's sharp cries to return. White Fang forgot that the gods had to be obeyed, and he soon found himself being pulled aboard Gray Beaver's canoe.

The Indian began to beat him, and White Fang's terror quickly changed to anger. His snarls made Gray Beaver more furious and the Indian began beating him harder and harder.

He beat him so hard that White Fang finally began to cry and yelp. Gray Beaver flung him down into the bottom of the canoe and picked up his paddle to row back to shore. But White Fang was in his way, and he kicked the cub savagely with his foot. This enraged the cub again, and he sank his teeth into the Indian's moccasined foot.

The Terrified Cub Jumped Into the Water.

# WHITE FANG

The beating that followed made the earlier one seem like nothing, for Gray Beaver was now beating him with the paddle as well as his hand. White Fang's fear became more terrible than anything he had ever known! But with that fear came another lesson—no matter what happened, he must never dare bite the god who was master over him.

When Gray Beaver reached shore, he flung White Fang onto the bank, where the cub lay whimpering and trembling. Lip-lip had been watching everything, and he pounced on the helpless cub and sank his teeth into him.

To White Fang's surprise, it was Gray Beaver who saved him. The Indian kicked Lip-lip high into the air so violently that the dog came smashing to the ground more than ten feet away. This was the man-animal's justice, and White Fang was grateful for it.

In the days and weeks and months that followed, White Fang often went to the edge of the woods to search for Kiche. He whim-

Gray Beaver Flung White Fang onto the Bank.

pered and wailed and cried, hoping that his mother would return, just as the man-animals returned when they went out hunting.

While he waited and hoped, White Fang's loyalty to Gray Beaver was growing. By obeying the man-god, he got extra pieces of meat. And he got protection from the other dogs' torments if Gray Beaver saw them attacking him or stealing his food.

These torments by the other dogs made the grief-stricken cub an outcast. The more he was tormented, the more wicked and ferocious a fighter he became. The more his food was stolen, the more cunning a thief he became. In fights with the other dogs, White Fang now always came out the winner. He never faced one dog alone; several always attacked him together. These attacks taught White Fang two important lessons necessary to stay alive: how to take care of himself in a mass fight and how to inflict the most damage on a single dog in the least amount of time. To

White Fang Always Came Out the Winner.

accomplish this, he learned to *always* stay, or land, on his feet, no matter how many times he was flung into the air or pushed back by heavier dogs.

He also learned that beginning a fight the way dogs did, by strutting around, snarling and bristling, served no purpose. But getting into the fight immediately, with no warning, surprised his opponent. So he learned to rush in, snap and slash, find the dog's throat, inflict quick and severe damage to its jugular vein, and get out, leaving his victim to die.

And even in these fights, Gray Beaver protected him from the anger of the dead dogs' masters.

So White Fang was now hated by both dog and man. He was greeted with snarls by the dogs and curses and stones by the man-gods. He always had to be ready for an attack, no matter where he went!

The other puppies always stayed together

Gray Beaver Protected Him.

in groups as protection against White Fang. They still chased him, but only in packs. If one dog ran ahead of the pack, the cunning wolf-cub would turn suddenly and attack, ripping the dog apart before the rest of the pack caught up.

If White Fang decided to trick them, he would run silently through the woods, listen for their noises, then make them lose his scent by crossing through water. How he enjoyed lying quietly in a nearby thicket, gloating over their confusion!

While growing up without kindness or affection didn't make White Fang's life a happy one, it did force him to become stronger, quicker, deadlier, more cunning, more agile, and more intelligent than the other dogs. He had to become all these things in order to survive in the life he was now living.

Growing Up Without Kindness or Affection

They Took Down Their Tepees.

# CHAPTER 7

## Loyalty and Rewards

When the summer ended, the Indians prepared to travel to their fall hunting grounds. White Fang watched carefully as they took down their tepees and loaded them onto the canoes. He was intelligent enough to understand that this was his chance to escape, to return to the Wild.

Some of the canoes were already out in the middle of the river when White Fang quietly slinked out of camp and headed into the woods. He hid his trail by crossing a stream before he entered a dense thicket, where he lay down to wait.

Hours passed before he heard Gray Beaver calling his name. White Fang didn't answer; he didn't move. And after a while, Gray Beaver's voice was gone.

At first, White Fang enjoyed his new freedom. But by the time night fell, he began to get lonely, and even frightened of the dark shadows in the woods. The air turned cold, and there was no warm tepee to snuggle against. He was hungry, and there was no piece of meat or fish thrown to him. He had grown so accustomed to living with the man-animals that he had forgotten how to shift for himself.

By the time daylight came, he had made up his mind to find his gods. He plunged into the forest and ran all day, with no rest. He followed a stream along paths where the land lifted up into mountains. He ran on thin ice that was covering a river, often crashing through and struggling against the current.

To Find His Gods

# WHITE FANG

He ran all night, smashing into anything in his path. But still he didn't stop.

By the middle of the second day, after he had been running continuously for thirty hours, his body began to weaken. He had not eaten in forty hours, the pads on his feet were bruised and bleeding, and his coat was stiff and knotted from repeated drenchings in icy water. Only his mind kept him going.

On the second night out, a thick snow began to fall. It was in this snow that White Fang found a fresh trail, one that he recognized immediately. He followed it to a camp, where he found Gray Beaver and his family. Mit-sah, his son, was cutting up pieces of moose meat; Kloo-kooch, his squaw, was cooking; and Gray Beaver was seated at a blazing fire, eating.

White Fang expected a beating as he slowly crawled toward his god. But there was no blow from Gray Beaver's hand. Instead, that hand offered him a piece of meat, then

White Fang Found a Fresh Trail.

another and another. And that hand also kept
the other dogs away as he ate. His loyalty was
being rewarded by his man-god with food,
warmth, and protection, rewards that would
soon come from his man-god's family as well.

In December of that year, Gray Beaver took
his family on a journey up the Mackenzie
River. On that journey, he planned to begin
teaching Mit-sah how to drive a dog team.
The seven puppies in the team were ready to
be put into a harness for the first time. Each
dog was attached to Mit-sah's sled by a different length of rope. This way, they ran
spread out, much like a fan, so that each dog
pulled as fast as he could without running
into the dog ahead of him.

Gray Beaver's journey continued for many
months, and White Fang was happy pulling
Mit-sah's sled as part of a team and continu-
ing to learn more about the man-animals'
laws. He already knew that dogs were never
to bite their man-animals no matter how

Teaching Mit-Sah How to Drive

much they were beaten or whipped. But during a stop at a village at Great Slave Lake, White Fang learned, to his surprise, that there were times when it *wasn't* a crime for a dog to bite a man-animal.

In this village, the dogs were allowed to go out on their own to search for food. One day, when White Fang was on a search, he came upon a young Indian boy chopping frozen moose meat. Chips of meat flew everywhere, with some landing in the snow at White Fang's feet. The wolf-cub ate those chips, then looked up. The boy had put down his axe and was coming at him with a club.

White Fang jumped out of the way and began to run. The boy followed close behind, yelling and swinging his club. The wolf-cub ran between two tepees, only to find himself up against a high mound of earth blocking his path. White Fang turned. The boy was between the tepees, blocking his escape, his club still raised, his eyes glaring furiously.

A Young Indian Boy Chopping Frozen Meat

White Fang bristled and snarled. He had done nothing wrong; why did this boy want to beat him? This enraged him so, that he leaped at the boy and sank his teeth into the hand holding the club.

What had he done? Ripping open the flesh of a man-god could mean a terrible punishment. He turned away from the wounded boy and fled to Gray Beaver's tepee, where he crouched at his man-god's feet for protection.

Moments later, the injured boy and his family entered the tepee and demanded revenge. Angry words and waving arms passed between the two Indian families, but Gray Beaver defended White Fang's right to protect himself against unfair treatment by other man-gods. So White Fang was not punished.

That same day, White Fang learned another law of his gods, one that concerned his god's family. Mit-sah had gone out into the forest to

He Leapt at the Boy.

gather firewood when he suddenly found himself surrounded by a group of boys from the village. Among them was the boy White Fang had attacked. Angry words were exchanged, then the boys began to beat Mit-sah with their clubs.

At first, White Fang sat and watched, feeling that this was a battle between the man-gods and so, none of his business. Then he suddenly realized that Mit-sah was one of his own gods too, and had to be protected. In a burst of anger, he leaped in among the boys. Minutes later, the white snow was covered with fleeing boys who left a trail of blood behind them as they hurried back to the village.

When Mit-sah told his story to his father, Gray Beaver rewarded White Fang with a large portion of meat. This, then, was another law—the law of reward for protecting his man-god's family.

The Boys Began to Beat Mit-Sah.

Return to the Village

# CHAPTER 8

# The Famine

Gray Beaver's long journey ended the following April, and he and his family returned to their village. White Fang was now one year old, and even though he wasn't fully grown, he was the largest cub in the village next to Lip-lip, and able to hold his own against any dog, even the full-grown ones.

Over the next two years, the dogs finally learned that White Fang's intelligence and cunning were superior to theirs and that it was much better to be at peace with him than at war.

# WHITE FANG

The year that White Fang was three, a great famine spread over the Mackenzie Indians. In the summer, there were no fish; in the winter, moose were scarce and rabbits had almost disappeared.

Hungry dogs battled each other, with the winners eating the losers. Old, weak Indians in the village died of hunger, while women and children gave up their food so that the men would eat and have strength to hunt. The famine was so great that the Indians ate the leather from their moccasins, while the dogs ate the leather from the harnesses on their backs. Soon, the Indians even began eating their dogs.

A few of the bolder and wiser dogs left the village and fled into the forest, where they eventually starved to death or were eaten by wolves. White Fang was among those that fled. He was better fitted for a life in the Wild than the other dogs, for he had lived that life when he was a cub. He knew

A Great Famine Spread

how to find fallen tree trunks or caves for warmth. He knew how to stalk small animals by lying concealed for hours, following their movements, and pouncing only when he was certain of success. He knew how to rob traps the Indians had set up, or outrun hungry lynxes or wolf packs, or attack and kill larger animals.

During the early summer, when the famine was nearing its end, White Fang came face to face in the forest with his enemy since cubhood, Lip-lip. The dog had fled the village the same time White Fang did.

White Fang was in splendid condition; his hunting had been good and he had been eating well for a full week. Lip-lip, however, had not been as successful in his hunt for food, and he was thin and weak from hunger.

Seeing his hated enemy before him, White Fang bristled and snarled. Lip-lip tried to back away, but White Fang was too swift. He struck him hard, throwing him to the ground

Face to Face with His Enemy

and rolling him over on his back. The next moment, White Fang drove his teeth into Lip-lip's scrawny throat. The death struggle was not much of a struggle, and in minutes White Fang had taken his final revenge on Lip-lip, repaying him for all the years of torment and suffering!

One day, not long afterward, White Fang came to the edge of the forest, where the land sloped down to the Mackenzie River. In a clearing, he came upon a familiar sight. It was his old Indian village, but in a new place. It had old, familiar smells of food cooking and old, familiar sounds of children laughing and women scolding. The famine was gone.

White Fang trotted to Gray Beaver's tepee, where Kloo-kooch welcomed him with happy cries and a large, fresh-caught fish. He was home; he was contented. He lay down to wait for his man-god's return.

His Old Indian Village

He Had Been Made Leader

# CHAPTER 9

## Beauty Smith, The Mad God

Over the next two years, White Fang became the most hated and the most feared animal in the village. He was hated because he had been made leader of the dog-sled team, and the other dogs were jealous of him.

He was feared because of his strength and speed and cunning. His brain and body were better coordinated than any dog's in the village; he attacked without warning and always destroyed his enemies before they knew what was happening, without ever being knocked off his feet himself!

# WHITE FANG

Stories of White Fang's ferocious fighting spread to other villages along the Mackenzie and even as far away as the Yukon Territory. Gray Beaver was fiercely proud of his dog. In the early winter of 1897, when White Fang was five years old, Gray Beaver heard that thousands of gold prospectors were heading up the Yukon River to Dawson and the Klondike. Knowing that they would need supplies, Gray Beaver spent the winter and spring hunting for furs and making mittens and moccasins to sell or trade.

With White Fang at the head of his dog-sled team, Gray Beaver reached Fort Yukon in the summer of 1898. It was here that White Fang saw his first white men. He realized that they were gods too, even stronger than his Indian gods. They had big houses and got on and off bigger boats. Because he was suspicious of them as well as curious, he always watched them from a distance.

White Fang's wolflike appearance made the

They Reached Fort Yukon.

white men curious about him as well, though none of them tried to come near or touch him at first. Later, when any of them did, he snarled, showed his teeth, and they backed away.

Many dogs lived at Fort Yukon. There were Indian dogs that were familiar to him, as well as those that came on the steamer with their owners. These dogs didn't impress White Fang; they were all shapes and sizes, and most were covered with hair instead of the fur they'd need in the cold North.

And none of them knew how to fight! Even though they were eager to attack him when they came ashore, and usually did, they were too soft and too helpless to win. They were no match for White Fang.

But the cunning wolf-dog also saw how angry the owners became when he killed their dogs. And since these fights were only a game to White Fang, he changed his strategy. He stayed in a fight just long enough to render the dog helpless, then trotted away

Many Dogs Lived at Fort Yukon.

and let the pack of waiting Indian dogs go in for the kill.

Many of the owners shot these Indian dogs, but White Fang didn't care. He had no loyalty to them, so it didn't matter what the white men did. However, he was impressed with the power of the white men's revolvers.

White Fang spent his time playing these fighting games at the steamer landing since there was no work for him to do. Gray Beaver was busy trading and getting richer every day. He had hoped to make a one-hundred percent profit from his trading, but instead was making *one-thousand!*

The men who lived at Fort Yukon enjoyed watching White Fang's savage and cunning fighting games. But one man enjoyed it more than the rest and even jumped into the air, whooping with delight, when the fangs of the pack dug into their victim's throat. This man was "Beauty" Smith. No one at the fort knew his first name, but everyone knew that his

He Was Impressed With the Revolvers.

nickname came from the exact opposite of his appearance, for he was probably the most "unbeautiful" creature on earth!

He was a small man with an even smaller head that came to a point. He had, in fact, been called "Pinhead" when he was a boy. His eyes were so spread apart that two other eyes could have fit in across the bridge of his nose. Above those eyes and along the sides of his head sprouted bunches of dirty yellow hair. All this ended in a huge jaw that seemed to rest on his chest because his thin neck couldn't hold it up. In short, Beauty Smith was a monstrosity!

Although he was a sniveling coward and a weakling, Beauty Smith was tolerated at the fort because he did the cooking and the dish-washing for the other men. But they also feared him and his rages, never knowing when he might shoot them in the back or poison their coffee.

This, then, was the man who admired

Beauty Smith

# WHITE FANG

White Fang, who delighted in his ferocity, and who swore that he would own him one day. When Smith tried to approach White Fang in the street, the dog ignored him. He didn't like the man and seemed to sense the evil in him.

White Fang was in Gray Beaver's camp when Beauty Smith first visited it. At the man's approach, the dog slid away to the edge of the woods, where he could watch the two men talking. When Smith pointed to him, White Fang began to snarl.

Gray Beaver refused to sell White Fang. He didn't need the money since he was now very rich from his trading. Besides, White Fang was the strongest sled-dog he had ever owned and the best pack leader and the best fighter. No, he was not for sale at any price!

But Beauty Smith was tricky and he knew the weaknesses some people had. So, he began visiting Gray Beaver, carrying a hidden bottle of whiskey under his coat. Smith knew exactly how to persuade Gray Beaver to taste

White Fang Began to Snarl.

the whiskey, then drink more and more until the Indian began to depend on it . . . until he began to crave it. Then Smith began charging Gray Beaver for the whiskey, charging more and more until the Indian agreed to pay any price for more of it.

Soon, all the money Gray Beaver had earned was gone, and he was left with an insane craving for more and more whiskey. That was when Smith asked him again to sell White Fang. This time, the price was not in money but in bottles. And this time, Gray Beaver agreed to anything to get more whiskey, even sell White Fang.

As soon as the whiskey was in his tepee, Gray Beaver tied a leather thong around White Fang's neck and handed the other end to Beauty Smith. Smith stood over them and began to bring his hand down toward the dog's head. White Fang's snarls grew louder to warn that hand away, but it kept coming until he snapped his powerful jaws. His teeth

All the Money Was Gone

closed down on empty air as Smith jerked back, frightened and angry.

But Beauty Smith was not to be stopped. He picked up a heavy club in one hand and tugged at the thong with the other. White Fang hurled himself at the evil stranger who was trying to drag him off, but this time, Smith didn't jump away in fear. He brought the club down on White Fang's head as Gray Beaver laughed and nodded his approval.

Dizzy from the blow, White Fang slowly crawled to his feet. He was wise enough to know that this white god was too powerful to be beaten... at least for now.

Once at the fort, Smith tied White Fang to a fence post and went to bed. Minutes later, the dog brought his teeth down on the thong and cut it in two. He trotted back to Gray Beaver's camp where he belonged; he didn't owe any loyalty to the evil white god.

The next morning, Gray Beaver turned White Fang over to Beauty Smith again. This

But Smith Was Not to be Stopped.

time, Smith used a club and a whip to give White Fang the most terrible beating of his life. The evil man's eyes gleamed with delight as he heard White Fang's cries of pain. For Smith was a coward and a weakling, and he took his cruel pleasure in beating any creature smaller and weaker than himself.

White Fang knew why he was being beaten. His old god wanted him to go with this new god, and his new god wanted him to stay tied up at the fort. He had disobeyed both gods and was now being punished for it.

But even this terrible punishment didn't stop him, and the following night he cut himself free again.

Although White Fang was wise, he was not wise enough. For he returned again to Gray Beaver, who had betrayed him twice. But he was a faithful dog, and for this faith, he was betrayed and beaten for a third time, even more terribly than before.

By the time the beating was over, White

He Cut Himself Free Again.

Fang was a very sick dog. A weaker animal would have died from Smith's beatings, but not White Fang. He couldn't move for hours afterward, but finally, bleeding and almost blind, he was dragged back to the fort and tied up with chains.

A few days later, a sober and penniless Gray Beaver left Fort Yukon on the long journey back to his village. He left behind a dog whose new owner was more than half mad and all brute!

To White Fang, Beauty Smith was a terrible god, a mad god, but still a god who had to be obeyed.

Back to the Fort

Chained in a Pen

# CHAPTER 10

## "The Fighting Wolf"

Chained in a pen at the rear of the fort by a mad god who teased and tormented and laughed at him, White Fang became a fiend, madder than his mad god. He hated everything and everybody: his chain, his pen, the men who peered in, their snarling dogs. But most of all, he hated Beauty Smith!

White Fang soon discovered that this evil man had a purpose behind this cruelty, a purpose that would satisfy his craving for blood and his craving for money!

One day, Smith entered the pen, unlocked

White Fang's chain, then hurried out. As a
mob of cheering men watched, he opened the
door again and another man pushed a huge
dog inside. Then Smith joined the men gathered outside and took their bets on the fight.

White Fang, himself, was over five feet long
and weighed ninety pounds, but he had never
seen a dog as huge as this mastiff. Enraged
over having been chained up, he now had a
living thing to vent his rage on. He leaped at
the mastiff and in a flash, ripped open the
side of the animal's neck. The mastiff lunged
at White Fang, but missed.

Back and forth they went, attacking, ripping, leaping, as the men cheered and hollered
and increased their bets. In the end, the
mastiff was defeated. Beauty Smith pulled
him out of the pen and greedily collected his
winning bets.

In the days and weeks that followed, White
Fang defeated all the dogs that Smith threw
into his pen, first one at a time, then two

The Mastiff Lunged at White Fang.

at a time, then three. Smith even brought in a full-grown wolf fresh from the Wild. No matter how terrible the fight, White Fang always came out the winner. He began to get a reputation as "The Fighting Wolf."

In the fall of the year, Beauty Smith took White Fang on a steamboat up the Yukon River to Dawson. There, he charged fifty cents for men just to look at White Fang. It didn't matter if the dog was asleep or awake, Smith would poke him with a sharp stick to get him in a rage, for an enraged dog made for a more interesting show.

But White Fang was also a fighting animal, and whenever a fight could be arranged, he was taken out of his cage and led off into the woods miles away from town. This was done at night to avoid detection by the mounted police in the Territory. Then, when daylight came, dog owners and gamblers would bring in dogs of all sizes and all breeds to fight . . . a bloodthirsty fight to the death!

White Fang—"The Fighting Wolf"

# WHITE FANG

White Fang's experience in fighting was far greater than that of any dog that faced him in Dawson. His early training against Lip-lip and the other puppies in the Indian village prepared him. So did the clashes at the steamer landing at Fort Yukon and the fights set up by Beauty Smith in the pen. When there were no dogs left to oppose White Fang, Smith started attracting crowds by pitting wolves and full-grown lynxes against White Fang. One female lynx was so ferocious that White Fang found himself fighting for his life. In the end, he won.

For months after that, the fights stopped, for there were no animals worthy of fighting White Fang. It wasn't until spring, when a gambler named Tim Keenan arrived in Dawson, that excitement began to build for the next fight, for Keenan had brought with him the first bulldog to enter the Klondike.

Would this be the final, fatal match for "The Fighting Wolf"?

A Female Lynx

He Stared at the Strange-Looking Creature.

## CHAPTER 11

# Rescued from the Jaws of Death

When the bulldog was pushed into the pen, White Fang didn't follow his usual pattern of attacking immediately. Instead, he stood still and stared at the strange-looking creature before him. The short, squat, clumsy dog was blinking and staring back at him as well.

Shouts of "Go get 'm, Cherokee!" came from the crowd.

But Cherokee didn't seem interested in fighting, as he blinked at the men and good-naturedly wagged his stump of a tail. He was really too lazy to be bothered with fighting.

Then Keenan stepped into the circle and began rubbing Cherokee's hair against the grain. This irritated the bulldog and made him growl. A strong push by Keenan sent him forward in a swift, bow-legged run.

Taking this as a signal to strike, White Fang jumped in, slashed with his fangs, then leaped clear and started circling. Bleeding from a rip in his thick neck, Cherokee calmly followed after White Fang, forming an inner circle to White Fang's outer one.

The cheering and betting among the men increased with each step the animals took.

Over and over, White Fang sprang in, slashed at Cherokee, and jumped back, untouched. And still his strange opponent followed after him, not fast, not slow, just in a deliberate, businesslike way.

This tactic puzzled White Fang. He had never seen such a dog, had never fought one who made no sound, and had never sunk his

This Tactic Puzzled White Fang.

teeth into such soft flesh. But the flesh White Fang aimed for, on the soft underside of Cherokee's throat, was out of his reach. The bulldog was too short for White Fang's teeth to reach *under* his neck; all he could reach were the sides, and these were already ripped open from his repeated slashings.

On his part, Cherokee circled around, waiting for the chance to fasten his deadly jaws on White Fang's throat.

Round and round they went, with White Fang often spinning around to change direction, leaping in, tearing at Cherokee, then leaping out. The bulldog followed, calmly taking White Fang's punishment while he waited.

White Fang tried over and over to knock Cherokee off his feet, but the bulldog was too close to the ground to be toppled. On his final try, White Fang drove his body against Cherokee's shoulder. Instead of knocking the bulldog down, White Fang tumbled over and across the bulldog's body.

White Fang Tumbled Over.

# WHITE FANG

The crowd gasped! For the first time in his fighting history, White Fang had lost his footing. He would have landed on his back if he hadn't twisted in mid-air to get his feet under him. As it was, he landed on his side, but was on his feet again the next instant. But that instant was enough for Cherokee's teeth to close on his throat.

White Fang tore around wildly, trying to shake off the fifty-pound bulldog clinging to his throat. Cherokee's dragging weight made him frantic. Round and round he went, but nothing he did released the bulldog's grip. He couldn't understand it. Never in all his fights had anything like this ever happened!

Out of breath and panting, White Fang lay down partly on his side while Cherokee tried to push him onto his back. The bulldog's jaws began opening and closing in a chewing movement, with each chew bringing those jaws closer to his jugular vein . . . to death! All

The Crowd Gasped!

that was saving White Fang now was the loose skin on his neck and the thick fur covering the life-threatening vein.

White Fang was having great difficulty breathing. This excited Cherokee's backers, who were already picturing the winning gold in their hands. This angered White Fang's backers, as they added up their losses.

Beauty Smith, however, refused to accept a loss. He had to make White Fang angry enough to continue fighting and he knew that exact way. He stepped into the circle, pointed his finger at White Fang, and began to laugh scornfully at him.

Laughter from a man-animal had always sent White Fang into a rage, and this time was no different. Mustering up what little strength he had left, White Fang got to his feet. Still dragging Cherokee's fifty pounds under his neck, he stumbled around the circle, falling and getting up, trying desperately over and over to shake off the death grip.

He Began to Laugh Scornfully at Him.

At last he fell backward, exhausted. Cherokee began to chew, shifting his jaws to bring him closer and closer to White Fang's jugular.

Shouts of victory went up from the bulldog's backers. But these shouts were soon interrupted by the jingle of bells and the cries of dog-mushers. The men in the crowd looked around, fearing the police, but it was only two men running with a dog-sled.

The men stopped their dogs and came over to join the crowd, curious to see what the excitement was all about. The dog-musher was a dark-haired young man with a mustache. The other, a taller, younger man, was light haired and smooth-shaven.

Beauty Smith paid no attention to the approaching men as he glared at White Fang. Realizing that the fight and his money were lost, Smith sprang upon the dog in a rage and began to kick him savagely.

By now, the tall young man had pushed

Two Men with a Dog Sled

through the crowd and was facing Smith, who was about to deliver another kick to the dying dog's body. The instant that he lifted his leg, Smith caught a smashing blow from the young man's fist in his face.

Beauty Smith fell over backwards and landed in the snow as the young man bent over the dogs and called to his friend, "I'll need you to pull when I loosen the bulldog's jaws, Matt."

"Coming, Mr. Scott," answered the dog-musher as he hurried into the circle.

When both men were in position, the younger man, Weedon Scott, tried to clutch the bulldog's jaws in his hands and spread them apart to release White Fang's neck.

The men in the crowd began to complain that their fun had been spoiled, but they stopped quickly enough when Scott glared up at them and warned, "You beasts! How could you stand by and enjoy this animal being tortured? I'll see that you pay for this."

Smith Landed in the Snow.

"It's no use, Mr. Scott," Matt said. "You can't pull 'em apart with your bare hands."

"We must, Matt. The bulldog's liable to reach the jugular vein at any moment."

Scott tried smacking Cherokee's head, but that didn't loosen his grip either.

"We'll need to pry his jaws open with something," said Matt.

Weedon Scott took his revolver from its holster and thrust the muzzle between the bulldog's jaws. He pushed and shoved until he heard the grating of the steel against the bulldog's teeth.

At that moment, Tim Keenan tapped Weedon Scott on the shoulder and warned, "You'd better not break them teeth, stranger."

"Then I'll break his neck," snapped Scott as he pushed the revolver in deeper.

"I said don't break them teeth," repeated Keenan, more threatening than before.

"If this is your dog, get in here and open his jaws!" ordered Scott.

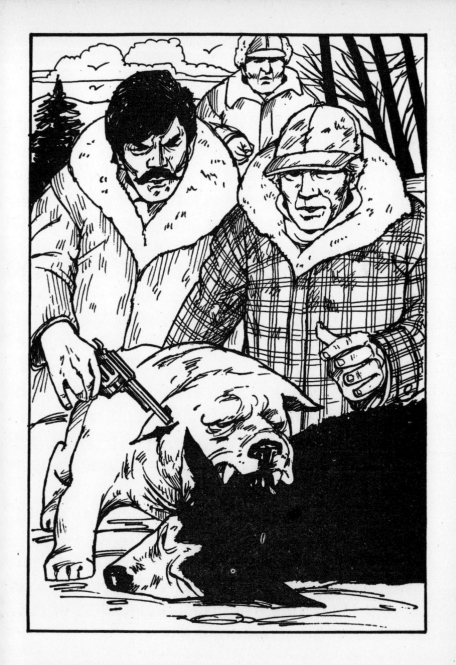

"You'd Better Not Break Them Teeth, Stranger."

"Well, stranger," drawled Keenan slowly, "I don't think I know how."

"Then get out of the way and don't bother me." And Scott went back to shoving the muzzle through Cherokee's jaws as a frightened Keenan backed away.

Once the muzzle was through, Scott pried open the jaws, a little at a time, while Matt freed White Fang's mangled neck.

"Now bend down and pick up your dog," Scott ordered Keenan, "and take him away."

Once Keenan had carried his struggling bulldog out of the circle, Scott and Matt turned their attention to White Fang. His eyes were half-closed and his tongue dangled limply from his mouth.

"He looks like he's been strangled to death," said Matt. "He's hardly breathin'."

Out of the corner of his eye, Scott saw Beauty Smith approaching. He said aloud, "Matt, how much is a good sled-dog worth?"

"Three hundred dollars."

"Pick Up Your Dog," Scott Ordered.

"And how much for one that's all chewed up and half-dead, like this one?"

"Half of that."

Scott turned to Beauty Smith and snapped, "Hear that, Mr. Beast? I'm buying your dog for a hundred fifty dollars." And he opened his wallet and counted out the money.

Smith put his hands behind his back. "I ain't a-sellin' my dog."

"Oh, yes you are!"

Smith began to back away as Scott sprang toward him and drew his fist back to strike him again.

"I got my rights," whimpered the cowardly Smith.

"You gave up those rights when you mistreated that dog!" shouted Scott. "Now, are you going to take that money or do I have to hit you again?"

"All right. But I take it under protest. That dog's worth a mint a-money. I ain't a-goin' to be robbed. A man's got his rights."

"Hear That? I'm Buying Your Dog."

"Yes," Scott answered. "But you're not a man. You're a beast!"

"I'll have the law on you when I get back to Dawson," threatened Smith.

"If you open your mouth, I'll have you arrested and jailed for running an illegal dog fight and betting on it as well. Or maybe I'll just have you run out of town," thundered Scott fiercely. "Understand?"

"Yes," grunted Smith as he backed away.

Scott turned to help Matt load White Fang onto their sled.

The crowd was beginning to break up when Tim Keenan pointed into the circle and asked one of the men, "Who's that guy, anyway?"

"Weedon Scott," came the reply. "He's a mining expert and an important man in the Territory. If you want to avoid trouble, mister, you'll steer clear of him."

"Yeah, I guessed he was somebody important," said Keenan smugly. "That's why I didn't fight with him right from the start."

Loading White Fang Onto Their Sled

"He's a Wolf. We'll Never Tame Him."

# CHAPTER 12

## Too Intelligent To Kill

Over the next several weeks, Weedon Scott and Matt nursed White Fang back to health at their cabin. As the dog's strength returned, so did his snarling, ferocious ways. He had been driven close to madness by Beauty Smith's maltreatment, so he had developed an intense hatred for all living things. As a result, he had to be kept on a chain so he wouldn't attack Scott's sled-dogs.

As the two men sat outside their cabin one day watching White Fang, Scott announced, "He's a wolf, and we'll never tame him."

"I'm not so sure about that," answered Matt. "I'd say he's been tamed already. Just look at the marks across his chest. They're from a harness."

"By gosh, you're right, Matt. He must have been a sled-dog before Beauty Smith got hold of him. Do you think there's a chance of his pulling a sled again?"

"He's still pretty wild now, Mr. Scott, but maybe I can start tamin' him if I unchain him and use a club."

"Then try it, Matt."

The dog-musher picked up a club and walked over to White Fang. "See his eyes followin' the club?" Matt called. "He's no fool. He won't attack while I'm holdin' it."

Scott watched as White Fang's eyes followed Matt's hand with the club. With his other hand, he unsnapped the chain.

White Fang could hardly believe he was being freed. Still, he was suspicious that these new gods were about to attack him or play

"Do You Think There's a Chance?"

some terrible trick on him.

He slowly and carefully walked to the corner of the cabin. Nothing happened. The men just sat and watched him. He came back and stopped a dozen feet away from them.

"Won't he run away?" Scott asked.

"We've got to take the chance," said Matt.

"That poor devil needs some human kindness right now," said Scott, as he reached into a bucket for a piece of meat. He tossed it to White Fang, but the dog sprang away from it, though he eyed it suspiciously.

The next instant, one of the sled-dogs sprang at the meat. Before the words, "Get back, Major!" had left Matt's lips, White Fang struck. Major's throat was slashed and his blood reddened the snow-covered ground.

Matt turned to White Fang and raised his foot to kick him. But with a leap and a snarl and a flash of teeth, the dog bit into the musher's leg.

Matt backed away and stooped to check his

"Won't He Run Away?"

bleeding leg. "He got me all right."

"I guess it's hopeless," said Scott with a sigh. "First Major and now you. There's only one thing left to do." And he drew his revolver out of its holster.

"Wait, Mr. Scott. That dog's been through hell. You can't expect 'm to come out of it tame as an angel. Give 'm time. And as for Major, why it served 'm right. He tried to take White Fang's meat and it's only right for a dog to fight to keep what's his. And as for me, I guess it served me right too. I had no right kickin' him either."

"I don't want to kill him," said Scott, putting away the revolver. "We'll let him run loose and see what kindness can do for him." With that, Weedon Scott walked over to White Fang and began talking to him in a gentle, soothing voice.

White Fang was suspicious. He had killed this god's dog and bitten the other god. What else was there now for him but some kind of

Talking to Him in a Gentle Voice

terrible punishment? But this god was approaching him without a club or a whip. Why? White Fang drew back as the god's hand reached out and slowly lowered toward his head. Was this a trick? A god's touch usually meant punishment. He snarled to warn it away. Still, the hand continued to lower toward his head. He didn't want to bite it, but his instinct was too strong. Striking with the swiftness of a coiled snake, White Fang slashed at Scott's hand.

Scott cried out sharply and grabbed his torn hand. White Fang crouched down and backed away, expecting a beating as terrible as any he had ever gotten from Beauty Smith.

Matt came running up to them, now with a rifle in his hand. "Just say the word, Mr. Scott and I'll kill 'm."

"No, you won't!" shouted Scott. "We're going to give him a fair chance. Besides, it served me right for approaching him this soon. Why, just look at him now."

## Was This a Trick?

# WHITE FANG

The men turned to stare at White Fang. He was now at the corner of the cabin, staring at the rifle and snarling viciously.

"Look at how intelligent he is," Scott insisted. "He recognizes firearms and knows what they're for. Now put that rifle away and let's give that intelligence a chance."

"All right, I'm willin'" said Matt as he leaned the rifle against a woodpile, then turned to look at White Fang. "Well, will you look at that!" he gasped in surprise. "He's quieted down and stopped snarlin.'"

Then Matt tried another experiment. He picked up the rifle again. And again White Fang started snarling. Then the musher raised the rifle to shooting position. White Fang leaped sideways behind the corner of the cabin out of sight.

Matt laid down the rifle and turned to Scott. "I agree with you, sir. That dog knows exactly what this rifle's for. He *is* too intelligent to kill."

"Look at That!" He Gasped in Surprise.

This Puzzled White Fang.

# CHAPTER 13

## The Love-Master

The following day, Weedon Scott came out of the cabin, his hand bandaged and held up in a sling. White Fang bristled and snarled at his approach, certain that he was about to be punished for biting the god.

The god sat down several feet away. He wasn't carrying a club or whip or firearm. This puzzled White Fang. Gods always stood when they punished him, and they always had weapons in their hands. Was this a trick?

His snarl softened to a low growl, then stopped as the god began to speak... calmly, softly, soothingly. No one had ever talked to White Fang this way before, and it had an odd effect on him. It gave him a feeling of security, a confidence in this god ... something he had never known with any other god. After a while, the god held out a piece of meat to him. White Fang refused to touch it from his hand. This could still be a trick.

Then the god tossed the meat on the snow. With his eyes fixed on the god, White Fang smelled the meat carefully, then took it in his mouth and swallowed. Nothing happened. The god held out another piece of meat, and again White Fang refused to take it. Again, the god tossed it onto the snow. This was repeated several times.

Finally, the god refused to toss the meat to him. He just held it out in his hand. The meat was good and White Fang was hungry. So, bit by bit, he cautiously approached the god's hand, never taking his eyes off the god, still not trusting him completely. With a low growl,

This Could Still Be a Trick.

he took the meat and ate it. Nothing happened. Piece by piece, he ate all the meat. And still there was no punishment.

All the while this was happening, the god went on talking softly and calmly. White Fang began to experience a feeling he had never known before... contentment.

Soon, the god's hand began lowering onto his head. But it didn't lower with a hard blow. Instead, it touched his fur gently. Still, White Fang growled a warning that he was ready to strike if the gentle movement became a terrible punishment.

The hand lifted and lowered, again and again, in patting, caressing movements. Soft words from the god's mouth accompanied each caress. White Fang had mixed feelings about this experience. It was against his nature to let anyone touch him, yet these touches produced a pleasant sensation, especially when the patting gently changed to a soft rubbing of his ears.

There Was No Punishment.

This, then, was an ending and a beginning
for White Fang. It was the ending of an old life
where he knew only violence and hatred, and
the beginning of a new life where he was to
learn love and devotion. But these were not
learned in a day. And *love* had to start with
*like*.

White Fang liked this new god, who allowed
him to run loose. This was a better life than
the one he had with Beauty Smith in a cage.
Besides, he needed a god, one whose life and
property he could guard.

He also lost his suspicions of the god's hand
and was soon enjoying its petting and caressing. Even his growls during these moments
were becoming softer and less fierce. And
Weedon Scott heard and understood this.

As the days went by, *like* rapidly grew into
*love*, and White Fang understood this too.
Having his god near filled him with joy.
Seeing his god go away filled him with pain.
But his god's return each night brought joy

An Ending and a Beginning

back into his life once more.

While White Fang *felt* this love for his god, he had never learned how to show it. He knew how to show anger and rage and hatred, but love was a new feeling for him. He had never barked in his life, so he couldn't greet his god with a bark of welcome. He never ran to his god, but rather waited at a distance to be called. The only part of him that was able to express his love for Weedon Scott were his eyes—the gleaming eyes that followed every move made by his love-master.

As he adjusted to his new life, White Fang learned to leave his love-master's sled-dogs alone. He also learned to tolerate Matt as one of his love-master's possessions even though it was Matt who fed him each day. However, he refused to let the musher harness him to the sled with the other dogs until after his love-master did it the first time.

Since White Fang was the strongest and wisest of all the dogs, he became the leader of

He Never Ran, But Waited.

the team. Even though he pulled the sled by day, he never stopped guarding his love-master and his love-master's property at night. To do this, he prowled outside the cabin while the two men slept inside.

In the late spring, however, his love-master disappeared. White Fang had no idea what was happening when Scott carried a suitcase with him as he left the cabin one morning. He only knew that his love-master never returned that night or the next or the next, although the dog waited for him out in the chill wind and driving snow.

When Matt came out of the cabin each morning, White Fang had no way of asking where his love-master was. He could only gaze at the musher with sad, lonely eyes.

Days came and went, and still the love-master didn't return. White Fang, who had never been sick in his life, became sick. He wouldn't eat, he wouldn't work. He just lay around on the cabin floor, lifeless.

He Lay Around, Lifeless.

Finally, in a letter Matt wrote to Scott, he told him, "That wolf wants to know what's become of you and I don't know how to tell him. Mebbe he's goin' to die."

One night several weeks later, while Matt sat reading, he heard a low whine from White Fang. The dog got to his feet and cocked his ears toward the door. A moment later, the door opened and Weedon Scott stepped inside.

White Fang stood waiting until his love-master called to him. Then he quickly came, his eyes shining brightly.

"He never looked at me that way all the time you were gone," said Matt.

But Scott didn't hear him. He was kneeling down, petting his dog, caressing his ears and neck and shoulders. And White Fang was answering his love-master's caresses with soft, happy growls. But something inside him told him he had to find still another way to show his love-master the joy he was now feeling. And he suddenly thrust his head forward

"That Wolf Wants to Know..."

and nudged it between his love-master's arm and body.

The two men looked at each other. Scott's eyes were glowing.

"Gosh!" exclaimed Matt. "That wolf really is a dog. Look at 'im."

Now that his love-master was home, White Fang recovered his health quickly. Within two days, he was his old, active, frisky self. Now that he had learned to snuggle and had experienced the close, secure feeling it gave him, he did it often.

Several nights later, Scott and Matt were preparing for bed when they heard terrified human cries and loud snarls from outside.

"The wolf's nailed somebody!" cried Matt, grabbing a lantern as they ran to the door.

Outside, they found a man lying on his back in the snow. His arms were folded across his face and throat to protect himself from White Fang's attacks.

The man's sleeves were already torn to

White Fang Recovered Quickly.

shreds and his badly slashed arms were streaming with blood.

Scott hurried to pull White Fang off the man. The dog struggled and snarled, but quieted down quickly at his master's voice.

Matt helped the man to his feet and pulled his arms away from his face. The ugly, evil face of Beauty Smith!

Matt pushed the man away from him with a hard shove. As Smith stumbled backwards, Matt spotted two objects lying in the snow— a steel dog-chain and a heavy club.

Weedon Scott saw them at the same moment. Kneeling down beside White Fang, he patted the dog and said softly, "Tried to steal you, did he? But you wouldn't let him. He sure made a mistake thinking he could take you away from me."

By now, White Fang's growls had taken on their soft, crooning note, and he snuggled his head in his love-master's arms.

Smith Stumbled Backwards.

"Just Listen to White Fang."

# CHAPTER 14

# A Long Journey Begins

Although White Fang spent most of his time outside the cabin, he had an uncanny sense of knowing what was happening inside. This would explain why he sat outside the door one day, whining and almost sobbing. Inside, the two men were making plans for Scott's return to his California home now that his work in the North was finished.

"Just listen to White Fang," said Matt. "I do believe that wolf can read your mind."

"Maybe so," agreed Scott. "But what can I do with a wolf in the South? He'd kill every dog in sight, and I'd have to sit and watch the police take him away and destroy him. No, I can't think of taking him with me."

"Certainly not," agreed Matt with a strange half-smile.

The half-sobbing whines and sniffing continued at the door.

"No denying he loves you," said Matt. "I never saw such devotion from a wolf."

"I know, I know. Now shut up, Matt. I know what's best for White Fang and me! Why, it'd be too hot for him," Scott argued weakly.

Weedon Scott's head had all the right reasons for leaving White Fang in the North, even though his heart wanted more than anything to take his dog home with him.

Finally, the day arrived that Scott was to leave. Through the open cabin door, White Fang saw his love-master's suitcases on the floor. He remembered staying behind on Scott's other trip, but somehow this trip seemed different... more ominous.

"I Can't Think of Taking Him With Me."

Matt looked out at the dog and commented, "From the way he acted the last time, I wouldn't be surprised if White Fang died this time. After all, you're leaving for good."

"Oh, shut up!" snapped Scott.

Soon, two Indians arrived and carried Scott's luggage out the cabin door and down to the steamer landing on the Yukon River.

The love-master bent down and gently rubbed White Fang's ears. "I'm hitting the trail now, old man, and you can't follow me on this one. Let me hear one last good-bye growl."

But White Fang refused to growl. Instead, he raised sad, longing eyes to his love-master, then snuggled his head in between Scott's arm and body.

At that moment, the whistle of the steamer *Aurora* sounded, and Matt called out, "You've got to be movin' now, Mr. Scott. You lock the front door and I'll lock the back."

Down to the Steamer

The two doors slammed at the same moment. From inside the cabin came low whining and sobbing, then deep sniffs.

"You take good care of him, Matt," Scott said. "And write and let me know how he's doing."

"I will, but listen to that, will you! Why, he's howling like dogs do when their masters die. I can't say that I ever heard such misery and grief from an animal."

Another whistle sent the men hurrying down to the river. As they boarded the *Aurora*, they found the deck jammed with both happy, successful gold-seekers as well as those who had gone broke searching.

Near the gangplank, Scott was shaking hands with Matt as the musher prepared to go ashore. Suddenly, Matt's hand dropped from Scott's grasp as he gazed at the deck behind his friend. Sitting there was White Fang!

"Did you lock the front door?" Matt asked.

Scott nodded. "And the back?"

Sitting There Was White Fang!

"You bet I did. But don't worry. I'll take him ashore with me."

Matt took a few steps toward White Fang, but the dog slid away, ducking and dodging between men's legs to avoid capture.

But when his love-master called, White Fang came immediately. Scott had bent down to pat the dog when he noticed fresh cuts on his muzzle and a gash between his eyes.

Matt bent down too and ran his hand along White Fang's belly. "We forgot about the window. He's all cut up under here too. He must've jumped plumb through the window, glass and all."

The steamer's final whistle sounded just as Matt was about to tie his bandanna around White Fang's neck to lead him off the ship.

Suddenly, Scott grabbed his hand. "Goodbye, old man. Oh, and about the wolf, you won't need to write. I'm ... Oh, shucks, *I'll* write to *you* about him."

"We Forgot About the Window."

Powerful and Wondrous Things

# CHAPTER 15

# Life at Sierra Vista

When the *Aurora* landed in San Francisco, White Fang was awed, yet a little frightened at the powerful and wondrous things the white gods had created: towering buildings, automobiles, horses pulling huge trucks, cable cars, and oh, there were so many white gods.

This nightmare lasted only a short time, for White Fang was led to a "room," actually the baggage car of a train, and chained in a corner. Several strong gods pushed trunks, boxes, and suitcases all around him. White Fang felt deserted by his master until he recognized the smell of Scott's clothes-bags and immediately sat on them to guard them, growling at anyone who tried to touch them.

An hour later, the god of the car opened the door and called to a man behind him, "I'm glad you're here, Mr. Scott. That dog of yours won't let me near your stuff to unload it."

Weedon Scott led White Fang out of the baggage car. The dog was astonished. The noisy city had disappeared while he was in that "room." In front of him now was a beautiful green countryside under a sunny sky.

White Fang saw a man-god and a woman-god get down from a waiting carriage and hurry toward his master. The woman's arms went out and clutched Weedon Scott around the neck—a dangerous act that could harm his master! White Fang began to snarl a warning.

Scott reached down to tighten his hold on the dog, as he said to the woman, "It's all right, Mother. White Fang thought you were

**"That Dog of Yours Won't Let Me Near Your Stuff."**

going to hurt me, and he won't stand for that. He'll learn our ways very soon."

Though pale and weak from fright, Mrs. Scott managed to laugh. "Then in the meantime, I shall just have to hug my son when his dog's not around."

"Not at all. Just watch." And he opened his arms to his mother while calling to White Fang, "Down with you! Down!"

White Fang had learned to obey this command though he watched carefully as the dangerous act was repeated. But surprisingly, no harm came to his master from that act, nor from the next one that was repeated by the man his love-master called "father."

Once the suitcases and clothes-bags were loaded into the carriage, the Scott family got in and off they went. White Fang ran alongside, snarling at the horses to warn them that no harm was to come to his god as they pulled him so quickly across the earth.

Fifteen minutes later, the carriage passed

"He'll Learn Our Ways Very Soon."

through a stone archway with broad lawns on either side. The carriage stopped when a sheepdog appeared in the road. White Fang's first instinct was to attack, but he stopped his rush when he realized that this dog was a female. His natural instinct would not let him attack a female.

But the sheepdog had no such instinct. She had a natural fear of animals from the Wild, especially wolves, since they had been attacking sheep as long as her breed had been guarding them. So, she rushed at White Fang and sank her teeth into his shoulder.

"Here, Collie!" called the man-god in the carriage.

"Never mind, Father," said the love-master with a laugh. "White Fang will learn to adjust to Collie."

The carriage started up again, but Collie blocked White Fang's path. He ran from one side to the other, but Collie kept blocking him at every turn. Finally, he turned on her and

She Sank Her Teeth Into His Shoulder.

knocked her to the ground with his shoulder, without hurting her. With the way now clear, he ran on ahead until he caught up with the carriage, which had stopped in front of the largest house he had ever seen.

Other strange gods came out of the house. Those in uniforms waited at a distance, but two women-gods ran to the master, repeating the dangerous act of clutching him around his neck. White Fang, however, was beginning to tolerate this act since it didn't harm his master. In fact, his master seemed to be enjoying it.

Then two tiny gods came running to join them. After clutching the master, they bent down to pat and hug Collie, who had caught up to the carriage.

The sheepdog was worried about the wolf. She was certain that her gods were making a mistake bringing him here to Sierra Vista, the home of her god, Judge Scott.

White Fang, however, knew that it was right

Repeating the Dangerous Act.

for him to be here with his love-master, and he quickly followed the family into the house and made himself at home.

Collie understood that her gods were protecting the wolf just as they protected her. But that didn't stop her from making his life miserable whenever she could in the days that followed. As for White Fang, he simply ignored her whenever possible.

White Fang came to understand about his master's family. Just as Gray Beaver had Kloo-kooch and Mit-sah as his possessions in his tepee, so did his master have his possessions in the big house. There was Judge Scott and his wife, the master's parents; Beth, his sister; Alice, his wife; and Weedon and Maud, his two young children.

Even though White Fang had disliked children all his life, hating and fearing their hands, he knew that four-year-old Weedon and six-year-old Maud were very much loved by their father. So, whoever his master loved

He Simply Ignored Her.

and protected, he must love and protect as well. Therefore, he did not growl or snap when their tiny hands caressed him. In time, he even grew to like them, welcoming them with a glow in his eyes when they came to play and looking after them with regret when they left him to play elsewhere.

White Fang allowed all the members of the family to pet him and fuss over him, but he never snuggled against them. He also never gave them his special love-croon; he saved those only for his love-master.

Outside the house, White Fang had much to learn. He learned most of it through his master's voice, but occasionally he had to learn something through a light slap of his master's hand. Because of White Fang's great love for his master, even this light slap from him hurt more than any beating Gray Beaver or Beauty Smith had ever given him.

White Fang had lived his life under the laws of the North, where all animals in the

Welcoming Them When They Came to Play.

# WHITE FANG

Wild could be eaten. So he assumed he could do the same thing here in the South as well.

Early one morning when White Fang came upon a chicken that had escaped from its coop, he followed his natural instinct and scooped up and ate the fat, tender bird.

Later in the day, he found another stray chicken near the stables. Before he had a chance to attack, one of the stable grooms ran to the rescue, swinging a buggy-whip. When the whip cut across his back, White Fang left the chicken and attacked the man, leaping for his throat. The frightened man raised his arm to protect himself, and White Fang's teeth sank into it.

Just then, Collie came into the yard and rushed at White Fang in a rage. She kept up her attack until White Fang had fled across the yard and into the fields.

When Weedon Scott learned what happened, he realized that the only way he could teach White Fang right from wrong was to catch him

He Followed His Natural Instinct.

in the act. That opportunity came two nights later when White Fang sneaked into the coop and attacked fifty white Leghorn chickens.

The following morning, when Scott saw the slaughter, he whistled in surprise, then chuckled silently in admiration. White Fang stood beside him, completely unaware that he had done anything wrong.

Mustering up all the anger and harshness he could put into his voice, Scott held White Fang's nose against the dead chickens and smacked him soundly. Then he took him into the yard where the chickens strayed. When White Fang made a move to attack one, his master's voice stopped him on the spot.

"You can never cure chicken-killers once they get the taste of blood," insisted Judge Scott at lunch when his son told the family about the lesson he had taught White Fang.

But Weedon didn't agree. "I'll tell you what I'll do, Father. I'll lock White Fang in with the chickens all afternoon. For every

Scott Whistled in Surprise.

chicken he kills, I'll pay you a one-dollar gold coin."

"Then Father should pay you, too, if *you* win," suggested his sister Beth. And everyone at the table agreed.

"But there's more, Father," added Weedon. "For every ten minutes White Fang spends there without harming any chickens, you'll have to admit, in your best judge's voice and in front of the whole family, 'White Fang, you are smarter than I thought.'"

So, after lunch, the family hid and watched White Fang in the yard. But he ignored the chickens, and lay down and went to sleep. When he awoke at four o'clock, he gave a running leap up to the roof of the chicken coop, then jumped down to the ground and trotted back to the house.

The family followed him and sat down on the porch. Judge Scott faced White Fang and, to the delight of his family, spoke slowly and seriously, saying sixteen times, "White Fang,

"White Fang, You Are Smarter than I Thought."

you are smarter than I thought."

White Fang learned other lessons when he was in town with his master. He wasn't to touch the meat hanging in butcher shops or attack cats and dogs who lived at houses his master visited or snap at people on the street who wanted to pat him or jump on boys who threw stones at him as he ran behind his master's carriage.

However, he also learned that his master protected him in these situations as well. One day, after he had been hit by a barrage of stones, Weedon Scott jumped down from the carriage and gave the stone-throwing boys a beating with his whip. After that, they never threw stones again.

Another time, he passed a saloon where three dogs had always rushed out to attack him, encouraged by their masters who thought it was great fun. Finally, Scott lost his patience. He stopped the carriage and told White Fang, "Go get them, old fellow."

"Go Get Them, Old Fellow."

# WHITE FANG

White Fang couldn't believe his ears. He looked at the dogs, then back at his master.

"Go get them, old fellow. Eat them up."

White Fang turned and leaped in among the dogs. There were snarls and growls and a clashing of teeth for a few minutes. Then two dogs lay dead in the dirt, and the third was fleeing down the road. White Fang gave chase and, with wolf speed, dragged him down and killed him.

After that day, word spread across the entire valley about the skill of the Fighting Wolf, and no man ever encouraged his dog to attack White Fang again.

White Fang Leaped in Among the Dogs.

Running Alongside His Master's Horse

# CHAPTER 16

# A Heroic Act

White Fang's life at Sierra Vista was happy. There was plenty of food and plenty of time to spend with his beloved master. The only nuisance in his life was Collie, who never gave him a moment's peace. So White Fang always pretended to be asleep whenever he saw her coming.

One of White Fang's chief duties was to accompany his master when he went out riding, running alongside his master's horse without ever tiring.

Riding was responsible for White Fang's

learning to bark—a sound he was to make only once in his entire life.

It happened one day when his master was out riding and a jackrabbit suddenly jumped under the horse's feet. The horse stumbled and fell, throwing Scott to the ground with a broken leg.

White Fang sprang at the horse's throat to punish him, but stopped when his master commanded, "Home! Go home!"

White Fang refused to desert his master.

Scott searched his pockets for a pencil and paper to send a message home, but found none. And again he ordered, "Home!"

White Fang didn't move. He just stood whining and looking sadly at his master.

Then his master's voice became gentle. "It's all right, old fellow. Go on home and tell them what's happened to me. Get along home, White Fang."

White Fang understood the meaning of "home" even though he didn't understand the

The Horse Threw Scott to the Ground.

rest of his master's message. So he trotted away, stopping every few steps to look back over his shoulder, hating to leave his god.

The family was on the porch when White Fang arrived, panting and covered with dust.

The children ran to greet him with glad cries, but he avoided their outstretched arms and trotted down the porch, growling.

Their mother called them away, fearful that the wolf would hurt them. The judge agreed.

"But he's not all wolf," argued Beth, much as her brother would have argued in defense of White Fang.

"Still," insisted the judge, "Weedon is only guessing that there's some dog in—"

But before the judge could finish, White Fang stood before him and growled fiercely.

"Go away! Lie down!" he ordered.

White Fang turned away from Judge Scott and went to his master's wife. He seized her dress in his teeth and tried to drag her off the

The Children Ran to Greet Him.

porch. She screamed in fright and pulled away from him.

By now, White Fang had stopped growling. Instead, he seemed to be struggling to make a sound with his throat, a sound these gods would understand . . . a sound their dogs made.

"Why, I believe he's trying to speak," Beth announced.

At that moment, the sound he had been struggling to make came to White Fang, and he let out a great burst of barking.

"Something's happened to Weedon!" Alice cried. "That's what White Fang is trying to tell us."

They were all on their feet now, following White Fang as he ran down the porch steps and across the lawn. As he headed into the woods, White Fang kept looking back to see that they were following him.

As a result of his heroic act that day, White Fang found a warm place in the hearts of everyone at Sierra Vista.

"I Believe He's Trying to Speak."

# WHITE FANG

By his second winter in California, White Fang made a surprising discovery. Collie was no longer attacking him with sharp bites. Instead, she was nipping at him playfully and gently, and he was becoming playful in return... though he felt ridiculous doing it.

One day, Collie led White Fang off on a long chase into the woods. Even though it was the afternoon that he was to ride with his master, White Fang was suddenly aware that a stronger instinct was telling him to go with Collie. It was the same mating instinct that had sent Kiche into the woods with One Eye years before... the mating instinct that had created *his* very life... the mating instinct that would one day create a new life from Collie and White Fang.

He Was Becoming Playful in Return.

Newspaper Stories of a Daring Escape

## CHAPTER 17

## "The Blessed Wolf"

It was about this time that the newspapers were full of stories about a daring escape from San Quentin prison. The convict, Jim Hall, was a cruel beast of a man, who was in prison for the third time, serving a fifty-year sentence for murder. During his escape, he killed three guards and stole their guns.

Hall was now the object of a manhunt all along the Pacific coast. Rewards were being offered. Bounty hunters were searching. Interest was high throughout California, but especially at Sierra Vista, for just before his retirement, Judge Scott was the man who had handed down Hall's sentence. And Hall had sworn that he'd take his revenge on the judge who sentenced him to a "living death!"

The women in the Scott family were frightened, but the judge laughed at their fears. White Fang knew nothing of this, but he did know that he shared a secret with his love-master's wife.

Each night after everyone was asleep, Alice Scott let White Fang into the house to sleep in the big hall. Since White Fang was not a house dog and so not permitted to sleep indoors, she awoke early each morning to let White Fang out before anyone was up.

On one such night while everyone slept, White Fang awoke and lay very still. He smelled the air and knew that a strange god was close by. Then his ears heard the strange god's movements.

White Fang didn't snarl or growl. He was too intelligent to attack this way. Surprise

White Fang Shared the Secret.

was more important. So, he silently followed the strange god's footsteps, walking more softly than the god did himself.

The strange god paused at the foot of the great staircase and listened. At the top of that staircase were White Fang's love-master and the love-master's dearest possessions. They had to be protected!

The god lifted his foot to the first step. It was then that White Fang struck! He gave no warning, no snarl, no growl. He just lifted his body into the air and landed on the strange god's back. There, he clung to the god's shoulders while he buried his fangs into the back of his neck. He clung for a moment, long enough to drag the strange god crashing to the floor.

White Fang leaped clear. But before the man could rise, he attacked with his fangs again.

By now, everyone at Sierra Vista was awake and alarmed. Standing at the top of

He Silently Followed the Footsteps.

the stairs, they heard horrible snarls and growls, screams of terror and anguish, the smashing of furniture and glass... and then gunshots!

After several minutes, the noises stopped. Weedon Scott pressed a button and the lights went on throughout the house. He and the judge started down, their revolvers ready.

But there was no need for weapons. White Fang had been the only weapon needed. For amid the wreckage of smashed furniture and broken glass lay the body of Jim Hall. His throat had been slashed open!

The men turned to White Fang. He, too, was lying on the floor. His eyes were closed and he tried vainly to make a sound, but a weak groan was all he could manage.

Judge Scott ran for the phone to get help, and in a short while, a surgeon was there, working on White Fang.

Hours later, however, the exhausted doctor came out and gave the family the sad news.

White Fang—the Only Weapon Needed!

"I'm sorry, but it doesn't look good. He has one chance in a thousand to survive. He has a broken leg and three broken ribs, one of which pierced his lungs. He's lost nearly all the blood in his body, plus he has many internal injuries. That beast Hall must have jumped on him. Of course, all of this is in addition to three bullet holes that went clear through him. . . . Did I say one chance in a thousand? . . . No, I'm afraid it's more like one in *ten* thousand!"

"We must try everything!" exclaimed the judge. "Never mind the expense. Bring in every doctor, every specialist, every piece of medical equipment in this country. White Fang must get every chance to recover!"

The surgeon smiled. "I understand, Judge. And I'll arrange for nurses to care for him night and day, just as we would for a human being, for a sick child."

The Scott women, however, insisted on caring for White Fang themselves.

"One Chance in a Thousand to Survive."

# WHITE FANG

For many weeks, the wolf hovered between life and death until finally, he won out on that one chance in ten thousand. After all, he had come from the Wild. He had inherited his strength and his will to survive from a strong wolf father and a courageous wolf-dog mother.

Still, he hated being tied down like a prisoner, with casts and bandages wrapped around him for weeks.

When the day finally came for the last bandage and the last cast to be removed, everyone at Sierra Vista gathered around. His master rubbed his ears, and White Fang crooned his love-growl. The master's wife called him "The Blessed Wolf," a name which all the women repeated.

White Fang was still very weak as he tried to get to his feet. He fell down several times, but refused to shame himself in front of his gods. So he tried again and again, until he stood on all fours.

His Strength and Will Came from the Wild.

"No *dog* could have done this!" exclaimed Judge Scott. "I still insist he's a *wolf*!"

"The Blessed Wolf!" cried the women.

"He'll have to learn to walk again," said the surgeon. "You can certainly start now. Take him outside. It won't hurt him."

So outside he went, surrounded by his gods and treated as a king. He was still too weak to go far, and he soon lay down to rest on the lawn.

After a while, little bursts of strength returned to his muscles, and he got up to take more and more steps after each rest.

When he had crossed the yard and reached the stable, he found Collie in the doorway. A half-dozen puppies were playing all around her in the sun. White Fang looked on in wonder.

Collie snarled a warning at him, and he watched from a distance. The master, however, used his toe to gently move one of the puppies toward him.

He Found Collie in the Doorway.

# WHITE FANG

White Fang cocked his ears and watched his son curiously. The puppy touched his nose to his father's, and his warm little tongue licked the big face above him. White Fang's tongue went out to lick the puppy in return.

The gods were truly delighted at this sight, and they clapped their hands and shouted cries of joy.

Soon, the other puppies came sprawling toward their father, much to Collie's annoyance. White Fang let his children tumble and scramble all over him as he lay with half-shut eyes, drowsing contentedly in the warm sunshine, surrounded by love.